FOURTEENTH WARD
COMMUNITY SAGA:

FOURTEENTH WARD COMMUNITY SAGA:

Reality, Hope, Dreams

CONRAD ALAN ISTOCK

authorHOUSE®

AuthorHouse™
1663 Liberty Drive
Bloomington, IN 47403
www.authorhouse.com
Phone: 1 (800) 839-8640

Published by AuthorHouse 04/19/2016

ISBN: 978-1-5246-0368-7 (sc)
ISBN: 978-1-5246-0366-3 (hc)
ISBN: 978-1-5246-0367-0 (e)

Library of Congress Control Number: 2016906131

Print information available on the last page.

Contents

Lorita, Looking Back. 1

Starting at the Gas Station, Detroit 1968............................ 8

A Mother's Dreadful Choice, 1971. 27

Charles's First Visit, from Chicago to a New Life, 1972. 37

A Disturbing Saga Unfolds, 2003. 44

Barton, a wealthy man, comes to Lake Union City............ 60

Emma's travail. 71

A Rescue, 2008. 80

The Restaurant Affair in 2010. 87

The Fight to Save the 14th Ward Schools, 2012. 91

Attacks by Bombers and Gunmen. 94

Lorita, Looking Ahead, Causes and Effects, 2021. 96

The Fourteenth Ward, Lake Union City, and all characters in this story are fictional, including Korean characters.

Lorita, Looking Back.

Let me introduce myself. I'm Lorita Harrison, Jason Harrison Junior's sister. Emma, our mother, is the wife of Jason Senior. I'm a social worker and historian in Lake Union City. After receiving my doctoral degree, I moved here in 1976 to be with my family. Over many years here, I have come to love this City, and especially our Fourteenth Ward. In the coming pages you will learn about my family, as well as many other fascinating people. For now, though, I just want to set the stage, so to speak, for the many, often surprising, places, and events to come—the stage on which all our joys, dreams, sorrows, struggles, victories, and passions play out. At the outset, I must add that in a number of places in this extraordinary development there will be unpleasant events and times.

I will start with some background information about this surprising Fourteenth Ward Community in Lake Union City. Then, I will lead you through some, though by no means all, of its early development, before turning to more than fifty years of striking, recent history involving its place in America and the World.

Lake Union City's earlier history came when runaway slaves first settled on a dirt road, with a few old, empty houses, running from the lake inward into the otherwise unoccupied Ward. That was about 1840. After the Emancipation Proclamation, and end of the Civil War, a few more free slaves joined them along with immigrants from some other countries and some poorer Ward residents. The free slaves and others supported themselves by working in agricultural fields. In 1900 that road was paved, and named Freedom Lane. And by then it was part of a much larger racially, and ethnically diverse community. Some descendants of the first slaves were later able to relate something about that early history when they met with the larger community at our beachside meetings every year.

The incorporated part of present-day Lake Union City proper has an area of about forty square miles, with about forty additional square miles of suburban or semi-rural political districts beyond. Overall, it is a fairly typical New England development, with the exception of the Fourteenth Ward, as will become clear as our stories unfold.

Lake Union City got its name because of two early glacial lakes on its west side. These lakes were originally filled with water flowing southward from the melting continental glacier receding to the north. The glacier eventually disappeared about 20,000 years ago. The two growing lakes were joined into a single lake by progressive submergence of a narrow, shallow connection between them that eventually reached a depth of about twenty feet, as it is today. Hence the name Lake Union City because it developed along the joined eastern shores of the two original lakes. The two large lake basins reach two to three hundred feet at their greatest depths. Across the Lake from the City lie natural forest slopes.

The Fourteenth Ward stretches narrowly for about eight miles along the eastern shore of Lake Union, and extends inward into the City for two to three miles. It is the original and oldest part of the City, and the only part along the Lakeshore. Development began in the late nineteenth and early twentieth centuries with quite large and elegant houses set back from the Lake along a narrow dirt road leaving a wide, and beautiful, natural area of scattered large trees and open spaces between the road and the Lake. Further development created more residential roads, eventually streets, inland with smaller, but still fine, houses. The first name of the area was Primrose. In 1910, when Lake Union City with multiple wards was created Primrose became its Fourteenth Ward. When the road along the lake was later paved it was named Primrose Street.

In the early Twentieth Century most of the Fourteenth Ward entered a steady physical and economic decline because most commercial and residential development went on inland, and because foreign immigrants, and particularly AfroAmericans, settled into smaller houses in many parts of the Fourteenth Ward. No doubt, cultural, ethnic and racial biases had a lot to do with the avoidance of the Ward by many, though not all, wealthier Caucasians.

Most prominent early on was the settling into the Ward of Middle Eastern families from Iraq, Syria, and Turkey in the nineteen twenties after the First World War. Unlike the present, angry, often violent interactions of the Muslim, Sunnis, Shiites, Alawhites, and others, did not occur. All got along well in the Fourteenth Ward, creating a sense of universal belonging that has helped the Ward avoid some later hostilities elsewhere in America. An area of restaurants and small shops along South Street, and a bank on the corner of South and Prospect Streets, became known as the Monsour District. It was named after that wealthier part of Baghdad, Iraq. Quite a few more people came to the Monsour District in the 1930s, 40s and 50s, along with other Middle Easterners.

During the period of the Ward's economic decline, real estate agents intentionally steered foreign and AfroAmerican customers to the Fourteenth Ward, and Caucasians, whether more wealthy or not, to other wards. The far eastern neighborhoods of Lake Union City soon became the areas of greater wealth. So, it became a segregated city in several ways. With similar dedication, realtors also steered wealthy, educated Caucasians to the suburbs. People of many more backgrounds eventually chose to live in the Fourteenth Ward: Korean, Chinese, Japanese, Italian, and more. Deterioration of property in the Ward continued to a lesser extent. Real change was coming.

Awareness of their depressed situation caused the Ward's people to talk a lot with each other, and they began to organize sometime around 1970. First, there were just friendships blossoming among neighbors of all backgrounds. During the 1970s wider groups formed clubs of many kinds, and in the fall of 1979 the first "All Community Gathering" on the Lake shore was organized by the newly formed Fourteenth Ward Citizens Association. Hundreds gathered with food, and music, and unending conversation, not to mention quite a bit of dreaming. Jason Senior and Emma arrived early that year to have their house on Primrose Street, just in time to be part of that Gathering. It was like a whole new life had opened up for them.

Those Gatherings continued every year, but much more was happening. Plans and money had been obtained to construct a waterfront complex farther up shore with docks, a swimming area, and a large picnic area. Next to it a small shopping unit of four stores for clothing, pharmacy, hardware, and foods was created.

Shortly after I arrived in 1981 my biggest surprise came at the third Community Gathering when I started talking with five teachers from all four schools in the Ward: preschool, elementary, middle, and High. These teachers were all excited about their teaching and the students. All had experiences elsewhere, but each said they had never experienced schools with this potential, such diversity, and near absence of discipline problems. One said; "The students learn so eagerly and fast, it makes my head swim. I have to work really hard every day to keep up with them." Two of those teachers had recently moved from across the City to the Ward. I realized two positives were at work here: The amazing diversity of student families and their backgrounds, combined with the attraction for really good teachers and administrators. Back then the quality of our schools was mostly unknown or denied elsewhere in the City, but that all changed as you will learn. And the result of that change will be some hard fought battles to keep our schools. At that Gathering I also met a very intelligent and charming professor at the Fourteenth Ward University named Sung who is the result of an amazing escape from North Korea.

This is not to claim that all will be positive with the Ward in the future. It will be surrounded, and at times hit, by the festering, often volatile, troubles that increasingly welled up in America, and the world, in the late twentieth and twenty first centuries. Still, what follows reveals the Fourteenth Ward in many dimensions, that for decades it has been a truly unusual place in America, and still is despite all the surrounding troubles in our Country and World.

I think the most remarkable, the most unusual, part of the origin and development of the Fourteenth Ward is the complex mixture of geographical origins, economic backgrounds, races, religions, and ethnicities that gradually came together over decades. It seems unique that in America such a complex, self-aware, and strikingly peaceful community should arise. Nothing is more striking than the diverse geographical origins of its people: from Detroit, Chicago, Minneapolis, Cincinnati, Middle East, North Korea, Central America, Asia, Africa, and others.

Now let us begin, in 1968, at our Dad Richardson's gas station in an economically depressed, impoverished, and racially isolated part of Detroit, Michigan, where Jason Jr and I grew up, when a horrible war abroad, Vietnam, was unfolding.

I'll offer a brief comment at the start of each of the episodes in this story.

Starting at the Gas Station, Detroit 1968.

Here we begin with events a long distance in space, time and culture eventually leading to the Fourteenth Ward. It makes clear how the surprising backgrounds of our family eventually came to the Ward.

It had been a quiet afternoon at the gas station in Detroit until two loud gunshots startled young Jason Harrison and his father Richard out of their chairs. They ran to the front window of the office. A short distance down the far side of the street they saw people on the sidewalk running away from the little convenience store. A black man with a pistol in his right hand rushed out of the store grasping his bloody right shoulder with his left hand. He ran with wobbly gait down the sidewalk, crying out in pain. Drops of blood fell from him as he rounded the next corner. The owner of the store came slowly onto the sidewalk holding his gun.

Richard chuckled, "Jason, that robber's a stranger for sure. Anyone living around here knows you don't try to rob Martin's store. Each day Martin appears old and slow moving, He looks helpless sitting alone behind his counter and cash box, but he always has his pistol, loaded and ready on that shelf below the counter. He never shoots to kill, though once he hit a robber in the heart by mistake, and that white guy got no farther than the curb. That man's death bothered Martin for months. He kept saying his eye caught something outside the window at the last instant and made his aim crazy."

They continued to watch as people resumed, moving almost normally along the street as a police car with siren blaring pulled up in front of the store. Martin, still on the sidewalk, started talking wildly with the two officers while he excitedly kept pointing in the direction the gunman had run. After five or so minutes writing their report, the officers climbed in their car, and raced off in the direction the robber had fled.

As Jason and Richard remained standing at the window it is striking how different father and son are. Richard is slender at six feet like the outstanding basketball player he once was, while son Jason, who plays football in high school, stands at six feet four with a build of solid muscle. They look different in other ways. Richard has very black skin, with numerous streaks of gray in his black hair, and he is clean shaven. A few soft lines cross his cheeks giving him a pleasant, reflective appearance. Jason is a lighter brown color with thick, bushy, jet black hair, a neatly trimmed mustache and beard. He looks younger than his eighteen years.

After the police drove off, Richard walked to his desk in a back corner and resumed sorting receipts. After a few more minutes watching people following Martin back into his store, Jason returned to work at a small table in the opposite corner next to the vending machine. He kept switching between work in his notebook, and staring out the window. Each time he looked out he was fascinated by the passing of old, rusty cars, and the variety of pedestrians of many shapes and sizes, both sexes, and a few children. Almost all were black, probably his neighbors, yet he knew only a few of them. He mused; *ours is a strange world where people live so near each other, in all these little old rundown houses jammed together along narrow side streets, with no real sense of a larger community. No way to join together and put a stop to crime, dirty streets, lousy schools, and all the rest. It so cheapens the quality of our lives. Does it really have to be this way?*

As a large, shiny, new-model limousine came swiftly toward the station Jason muttered: "Wow! A drug man or gun seller for sure." His father looked out at the limo just when it was right in front of them.

"What did you say, Jason?"

"Nothing really, Dad. I was just watching that fancy limo. Don't see many of them here."

"One is too many, son. You can be darn sure it's not the mayor or governor visiting us. Likely someone with a business that makes our neighborhood worse than it would be without him. I mean a guy like that who can afford a chauffeur, and the two bodyguards in there with him, is at the root of half our problems."

"Yea, that's what I suspected."

"Well, I suspect you're not getting that school work done. Just because its a little less than two months to graduation doesn't mean you can slack off. You are mighty lucky you got into Technical High School. Your success at that school is the reason Wayne State accepted you, and that kind of college education will make all the difference for the rest of your life. These are times when a black man with solid education can get ahead in the world. Not like it used to be. For years I feared that you and your sister would wind up in our ghetto high school. Before she died, your mother was your teacher, and she made up for the bad early years of grade school here. Bless her, dead now these three years."

"I know you're right. This is math and I have it under control, though I don't really like math or science. They're not about the real world, you know what I mean, about what affects everyday lives of people who can't afford leisure. Like most, if not all, of these ordinary people going by. I want to study things in college that make a difference for people."

No sooner had he turned back to school work, when his attention was grabbed by a car pulling alongside the gas pump. It was Garson's old Ford that he had repaired more times than he could remember. He watched his father walk out, pump the gas, and clean the windshield. Garson got out to pay. and the two men talked for at least ten minutes. He could hear them laughing once. They had been friends for years. One of the few neighbors you really counted on. As he watched them Jason recalled how Garson volunteered to help out at the station when Richard was in the hospital for his hernia repair five years ago, and that he was a pall bearer at his mother's funeral. A good man, but pretty much poor like the rest of us. But just like now, he almost always had that ready smile on his clean-shaven, chocolate-colored face.

Over the next hour light rain fell as dusk quickly descended. Three more cars came for gasoline. When the third customer drove out Richard turned off and locked the pump. The rain had increased, and it had gotten colder causing Richard to finish quickly and hurry inside.

"Jason, if you'll lock up in here and turn off the outside lights, I'll go back and fix supper. I'm taking the cash back to our safe. A little later I want us to listen to something on the radio that should interest you. It will probably have a lot more to do with your future than mine."

"What is it?"

"Just wait and see. Oh, by the way, I called Martin. He's alright. When he shot the robber that guy's gun went off, but his bullet just went into the ceiling, as he almost fell down before he ran out. That explains the two shots. I didn't think Martin would try to kill him."

Jason returned to school work. Soon the clinking of pans followed by pleasant odors from cooking hamburgers signaled that dinner would be ready shortly. Unable to resist he ambled back into the kitchen, and sat ready at the table. After a few bites he said. "Dad, what is this thing coming on the radio?"

"I just want you to hear it. It's really important."

With supper over Richard sat reading the paper as Jason washed up the few pans and dishes. At nine o'clock Richard turned on the radio.

An announcer started speaking about a recorded speech by the Reverend Dr. Martin Luther King, Jr. A speech he gave on April fourth 1967 at the Riverside Church in New York City, before a meeting of the Clergy and Laity Concerned. The group of Clergy were strongly in opposition to the ongoing war the U.S. had launched in Vietnam starting in the early sixties.

Before the recording started Richard's face had a look of sad seriousness. Watching him, Jason looked puzzled. They heard the hush of the crowd in the Church go almost silent as Dr. King began.

Richard and Jason listened mostly silently for almost an hour as Dr. King made it clear that it was no longer possible for Americans to remain uninvolved over the Vietnam war that was raging badly by this time. He praised a recent statement issued by the executive committee of Clergy and Laymen Concerned which he fully supported.

As he went on it became clear that he thought the War was a horrible mistake costing thousands of American and Vietnamese lives. He emphasized the difficulty that comes with opposing ones Government and President in times like this. He recognized that opposing ones Government over this war was difficult, but emphasized throughout the talk that it was now necessary. He admitted that he had been silent about the War over too many recent years, far too silent about all the violence and destruction we were causing in Vietnam. He stressed in many ways that the U.S. intentions in Vietnam were not honorable. He saw it as a war dedicated to the killing of the people of Vietnam, rather than having compassion, and regard for the views and aspirations of those unfortunate people, as well as their rising hatred toward us. He asserted that we wanted to make Vietnam a colony with the possible goal of drawing China into war. He closed with a short poem by James Russell Lowell.

After a long applause the announcer came on again, and told the audience that Dr. King had been assassinated in Memphis a few hours earlier after giving a different speech there. The noise from the crowd swelled into a volume composed of sounds of grief and anger for several minutes before the announcer shut off the broadcast.

Richard dropped his face down. Jason had never seen his Dad's face so sad since the time of his mother Marata's death. Even small tears in the corners of his eyes now were like ones he remembered at her funeral and burial.

Throughout the entire, long Vietnam speech, Richard and Jason had listened almost silently with only a few expressions of dismay or approval from Richard. And now there were many tears on his cheeks when he lifted his face.

"Most of it upset you, Dad, didn't it?"

"Yes. A lot, mostly because of you, I suppose, but also because of what is happening to our country and the world."

"Why because of me?"

"It's the troubled future you must face. The military draft. Any time soon you may be forced to fight there in Vietnam. In the paper here it says over twelve thousand of our soldiers have already died in Vietnam, and many more injured. This is hell! And being in college may not protect you from the draft as it did a few years ago. This is real hell! When we voted for President Johnson a few years ago he promised he would not send our boys to fight there. He lied to us, and now our boys, and lots of Vietnamese boys, and ordinary men and women, are dying for no good reason. Kennedy had said the same thing, and then sent advisors to Vietnam, and before him Eisenhower had sent a letter to the president of South Vietnam saying we would come to their aid if North Vietnam attacked.

"In 1942, when I volunteered, and went to fight in Europe, I knew it was the right thing. Hitler had to be defeated. Since then it has been two bad wars. Korea went badly, and is still a stalemate after all these years. At least it was an United Nations effort involving sixteen countries, to thwart North Korea's invasion of South Korea. This one in Vietnam was not necessary, and it sure looks like it will turn out badly, too. It's all our own country's stupid mistake. We had ample warning from the disaster that earlier befell the French army at Dien Bien Phu in Vietnam. Sometime you should read Bernard Fall's 'Hell in a Very Small Place' about that slaughter of the French troops in Vietnam in 1954. That alone should have told us to stay out. Bless King for opposing it, but now look at what that and all his other good work has gotten him. Dead, assassinated while talking to two friends outside his motel room.

"Anyway, it's bedtime. Maybe tomorrow will bring a few rays of hope."

Lying awake, Jason stares at the photograph on his bedside table—a photo of the four of them taken a few months before his mother died. His beautiful mother Marata and elegant older sister Lorita are lighter skinned, his father much darker, and he somewhere in between. Beside that is a photo of his mother and dad just after their wedding. He stares at the photographs for a long time and then thinks: Maybe dad is right. The future may be brighter for well-educated black people. Still, King's speech and things dad said make me wonder and worry about future possibilities. What lies ahead for Lorita in the Peace Corps? What is happening to our country and world? Where does my own future go? To war? While I'm in college I'll be here to help with the station. But, what if I go to Vietnam and maybe never return? I wish mother was here. I need her, too, now.

An hour passes until he falls asleep.

The last thoughts Jason had just before falling asleep returned as he awoke. As he lay there with the first light of dawn coming through the windows his mind reviewed all those things from the night before. Then he rose slowly, stretched, and went in the bathroom to wash up and comb his hair. He dressed quickly and went into the kitchen to make his breakfast. Sitting down with a large bowl of cereal, he watched as his father came in.

"Dad, I've been thinking a lot about what we talked about yesterday. I know for sure I don't want to go fight in Vietnam. When I get into college if the draft doesn't come after me, I'll be able to keep working here at the station and help you out. If the draft calls me, I'll need another plan to avoid it. Don't you think?"

"Yes. I really don't think there's much of a choice. If the draft calls, they'll come after you. I thought a lot about this several days ago. I called a friend of mine, Henry, who has a gas station in Hamilton, Ontario. He said that he would take you on to work at his station, and that you almost certainly could enroll at McMaster University there. Cost of the University would not be expensive, he thinks, and you could afford it with what he would pay you. Henry says it's an outstanding university. I will help you get there. If we had more money I might consider sending you off to Sweden or England where other draft dodgers have fled, but we can't do that, And selfishly I'd like to have you closer."

"Are you serious, you'd help me escape to Canada?"

"I'm dead serious. I can't allow you to go and fight in Vietnam, and even though you might enter the military and avoid being shipped to Vietnam, we can't take the chance. Henry says you'll need a passport, and we'll get that right away. He is certain he can get you a work visa when he certifies that you will have a job at his station. He thinks you will be able to get a student visa if the university accepts you. That would last for at least three years."

In midJune of 1972, at the end of Jason's senior year at Wayne State, and one day after graduation ceremonies, a letter came calling for him to report downtown at once for induction into the Army. Richard immediately picked up the phone.

"Henry, the worst has come. Jason is about to be drafted."

"Don't worry Richard. He can come here. I have plenty of work and sufficient money to pay him. Does he have a passport and a car, if no car he can take a bus?"

"Yes. we've got passports and an old, but worthy, car."

"Good. Tell him to cross over in Windsor early tomorrow and drive straight here, He can stay with us until we find an apartment for him. I have a friend who will help him apply for school here if he wants to enroll at McMaster."

Very early the next morning, Richard, driving his pickup, followed Jason in his old, red, Ford coupe until both had cleared customs. They stopped for breakfast at a small cafe in Windsor. As they finished their food and light conversation, Richard turned serious.

"Two things you must not do. Don't call by phone to my station. Don't send any mail to me there. The draft people will be looking for ways to track you down. Here is Garson's phone number and address. If you need to tell me anything, call or write him. If you send him a letter don't include your name and a return address, but I prefer you just call him. If you call him, do it from Henry's station, or if you get a phone number of your own in Hamilton, use a different name, something like James Maddison. I'll contact you at Henry's station, or at your apartment, using Garson's phone. That's how I can arrange to meet you somewhere along highway 401 occasionally. If Lorita's home. I might bring her along."

Jason couldn't keep from laughing. "Dad, this sounds like some sort of spy novel."

"It's not a joke! They'll try to find you and put you in jail. They've done it to a bunch of draft dodgers already."

"Of course, I believe you, and I'll be very careful. Actually, I guess I'd even worry they might try to follow you into Canada if we are set to meet on 401."

"I've thought about that, and it scares me, but I don't think they would. I could have Garson rent a car for me, and I'd leave from his house. We'll see. Now, you must get moving."

"OK. I'm ready. Thank you for this, Dad. Strangely, I think Dr. King might approve."

"Yes, probably. But give my thanks and best wishes to Henry Crawford when you get to his place. He and I go back a long way, but things have moved so fast I haven't had time to tell you any of that.

They paid the bill and walked out to Jason's car. Standing uncertainly for a minute they suddenly hugged each other tightly, repeatedly saying goodbye.

Jason got into his car and drove out of the parking lot. Richard watched the red coupe heading out of Windsor until it was no longer in sight.

Following the map of Hamilton that Richard gave him Jason reached Henry's gas station about five hours later. He parked near the office and stood uncertainly by his car for a minute or two. A tall, strong, white man came out and approached him.

"Hello. I'm Jason Harrison. I'm looking for Henry Crawford. Is he here?" Jason looked surprised when the man said.

"I'm Henry, and from the look on your face I suspect you were expecting a black man.

"Dad never said you were white. He just said you were a fabulous friend he met on the invasion of Normandy in the big war, and in all the fighting against the Germans after that. And that you have stayed in touch ever since."

"Well, come on in and relax a bit. I think I've found an apartment for you that is a short walk away. We'll go look at it after a bit. And we've got plenty else to talk about."

Jason continued to look at Henry with short glances. He was fascinated by his straight hair, a mixture of gray and blond. Equally surprising was Henry's neatly trimmed, blond mustache, blond eyebrows, and lightly tanned skin.

On Monday morning of the next week, two military officers walked into the station in Detroit and asked for Jason.

Richard knew why they had come and responded calmly. "He's not here. The day after his college graduation he and some college friends went on a celebration tour of Europe,"

"Well, you've got to call him. Tell him to fly back at once, and report for the draft."

"I don't know how to contact him. I think the group is traveling all over and mostly camping out. They planned their own six week excursion."

"Is he trying to dodge the draft? If so, it will mean jail time for him."

"He's not a draft dodger. The letter telling him to report came after he left. It's over there in a small stack of his mail."

Officers repeatedly came to the station during that summer. Often they vaguely threatened some sort of legal action against Richard for hiding a draft dodger.

"What can I do? I don't hear from him. I don't know where he is." He would always say.

By their agreement, Jason and Richard did not write or call each other, because they feared the authorities might be monitoring phone calls and mail coming to the station.

Indeed, that was exactly what was happening. Finally, after over a year the authorities gave up.

Jason worked at Henry's station for three years and studied at McMaster University in economics courses for two of those years. The Vietnam war ended in 1973 with the last US soldiers and citizens desperately fleeing from the top of the Embassy to an overcrowd ship bound for the Philippines. It was a repeat of the French soldiers trying to make a mad-dash escape from Dien Bien Phu years before.

In 1975 Jason applied for admission to the University of Michigan Business School and was accepted into their masters program. By that time the US government was no longer trying to catch and prosecute those who had fled the Vietnam draft. Two years later President Ford exonerated draft dodgers in general. The terrible war had taken many tolls, eventually military conscription, the draft itself, was one.

Very early on the first Monday of August in 1976, Jason packed his car and drove home from Hamilton, Ontario to the station in Detroit. Even though he had only been gone for a little over three years, his father looked much older to him as they hugged each other. Garson was there, flashing a big smile, as he wrapped his arms around Jason.

His face sad, Richard spoke softly. "Well, thank God you are alive, Jason. Tens of thousands of our soldiers have died for no reason over there,"

Garson shook his head in agreement.

"I'm alive thanks to you Dad, and to Garson and Henry for giving me a chance to live usefully through this period of national disaster.

Garson smiled again and said; "I'm going to Martin's store and get us some sandwiches and a bottle of wine for lunch. We need to celebrate."

The next Monday, Jason drove to Ann Arbor, found a tiny basement apartment, and enrolled in business school classes. A few days later he got a part-time job working at a small gas station close to the University of Michigan campus. In his second week after classes had started he was walking rapidly across campus to get to his job when he stopped suddenly to stare at a woman approaching.

"Something wrong?" The woman said, with a puzzled look.

"Oh no. For a minute I thought I knew you. I'm Jason Harrison, but I apologize for startling you."

"That's OK," she said as she moved past him.

As he moved on, Jason's thoughts were all about that woman. Amazing, I actually thought for a second it was my mother, Marata. She looks almost exactly like that photo of mother when she was just married.

Frequently, on following days they would pass each other. After a month, Jason got up enough courage to speak to her again. He was clearly uncertain and stammered a bit as he spoke.

"Excuse me, we pass often, I'd I'd like to know your name just to say he-hello. I'm Jason Harrison."

"Don't be so shy, I remember your name. I'm Emma, Emma Carson. What are you studying?"

"I'm in the business school, for a masters degree. What are you doing here?"

"I'm working on a Ph.D in literature and writing."

Like Jason's mother, Emma was beautiful with soft, somewhat lighter, brown skin. Her black hair fell gracefully below her shoulders with no indication of curls. She was slender and almost as tall as Jason.

They spoke often, and started dating after a few more weeks, and were married two years later when they both graduated. They stayed in Ann Arbor because Jason got a job managing a nearby car dealership. He moved up quickly, and was put in charge of three dealerships. Then, three years later he was hired to manage six dealerships in Lake Union City. His main office there, it turned out, was in the dealership in the Monsour district of the Fourteenth Ward.

While Jason was at Michigan and working in Ann Arbor, Garson helped out at the gas station. One day in 1977 he called Jason at work to tell him Richard had died of a heart attack right at the station. After the funeral, the gas station was sold because neither Lorita or Jason wanted to take it.

Emma had published three short stories, two poems, and was writing a novel when they moved to Lake Union City, and settled into a beautiful old house on Primrose Street in the Fourteenth Ward across from the edge of the lake.

Having finished her stint in the Peace Corps in 1972, Lorita enrolled at Wayne State, and earned a degree in sociology. She followed Jason and Emma to Lake Union City, taking a position as a Social Worker assigned to work with a large part of the population living in poverty with some homeless.

A Mother's Dreadful Choice, 1971.

Here we learn about the amazing way in which Sung, a talented child from North Korea, eventually comes to the Fourteenth Ward.

At daybreak, the old, rusty-gray bus rumbled over the gravel road and stopped near Kijong-Dong, North Korea's only village in the Demilitarized Zone (DMZ) adjoining South Korea. Despite pretense created by a towering pole flying the North Korean flag, the drab-white buildings in the village were far from finished. Seventeen years had elapsed since the initial construction. Yet, there was still no glass in the windows, inside walls had never been built. Only a few lights came on at night in one low, partly finished, building. Two armed soldiers, stationed on the entrance road day and night, were the only people seen in the village.

Workers descended from the bus. They picked up baskets, and spread out to harvest fresh vegetables, and ginseng tubers, for government markets in villages north of the DMZ. This day, like most, warm rays from the rising late-summer sun crept across the fields to meet them.

One worker, Angse, was different: clearly younger than the others at twenty three, short and slender, with dark eyes and hair, and an unusually pretty face. She wore a simple, but colorful blouse and head scarf, a brown sweater, and a skirt that reached her knees, unlike the trousers worn by all the others. She was strikingly different in another way. She had a small baby, asleep, and almost completely covered in a tan pouch hung against her back. She also carried a small satchel.

Angse always went to the far edge of one large field. On this first day she cast furtive glances toward other workers to see if they were watching her. Then she relaxed when they seemed oblivious to her and the baby. Each time she returned with a full basket and picked up an empty one she retreated to an area near the far edge of that large field. Late on this first day a tall, dark-haired man came to check on Angse and her baby. They talked a little about the difficulties of having a child with her, and the hard work in the fields. It was a gentle, warm encounter that made Agnse feel good and calmer.

After a few hours on her second day, two women approached Angse and asked if they could see her baby. When Angse opened the pouch to fully reveal the baby's face one woman exclaimed: "Oh. how beautiful. How special and charming. You are so lucky." These women offered to help her as the day wore on. In mid-afternoon a gray haired man approached her and talked with her for several minutes about how much his daughters and their babies meant to him. These friendly encounters occurred each day, and always gave Angse pleasant feelings, except that after each such occasion sadness would return. She would think; *our people are so nice and friendly, but why are all our lives so hard?*

Several times each day the baby woke, made pleasant noises or cried if she was hungry. Three times each day Angse moved out of the field into the shade of nearby shrubs and small trees, to nurse her baby. When needed, she would remove the diaper, take a small cloth and water bottle from her satchel, dampen the cloth, clean the baby, and put a clean, cloth diaper on her. Natural beauty at this spot appealed to Angse. There were three large shrubs with many deep red flowers, and small plants with bright yellow flowers covered the ground. Angse always tarried a few minutes just to talk softly to her baby. On the tenth day a woman of about fifty years with white hair came to Angse as she nursed the baby. They had a warm and wonderful exchange about the joy of bringing a new life, but as the woman left a sense of near despair swept over Angse.

For ten days Angse had come with her baby. Each day she thought she would carry out her desperate plan. Each day her anxiety grew. Still, by late afternoon she would say softly to herself; "I'll wait until tomorrow."

On the eleventh day, after a third feeding, her thoughts grew intense and scattered; *This has to be the day! We've been told to make tomorrow our last day here. After that we will be sent to fields farther north. I will never have another chance. Life for a growing girl in our poor village is no life at all. Hopeless. No opportunities to develop abilities and talents. No serious education. It took me years to learn some English from old newspapers left by travelers. We have little nourishing food for our children. No future in our country. I can't, I won't, let her face this awful life. My husband Cha doesn't like my plan, but still does not object. This has to be* the day. I'll do it.

Sadness nearly overcame Angse with this rush of thoughts as she stared at her lovely baby. Sweat broke out on her forehead. Then, as a look of determination seized her face, she strapped on the baby in its pouch and hurried back to work, again saying firmly to herself; "I will do it!".

The harvesting was hard and long that day.

When dusk descended, the driver honked three times to signal all should board the bus for the return trips. As others hurried onto the bus, Angse, standing at the far edge of the field, quickly moved into the woods. The driver was not checking if everyone was there. She had counted on this lack of checking, because the driver almost never checked. The engine started, and the bus lurched noisily up the road. She hoped they didn't notice her absence. Very likely they did, and said nothing. Though none of them knew of her plan.

She tried to recall all she had learned by studying maps of the DMZ—sometimes with thoughts about escaping to freedom. She recalled her experience one crucial lunch break five months earlier, while working these same fields during spring planting. She had gone exploring and reached the high wire fence with its great, frightening, spiral roll of barbed wire along the top—the daunting barrier separating North and South Korea.

At the so-called "Bridge of No Return" she had pushed the bottom of the fence next to a large post with her foot, and saw the fence would swing up and away slightly. She could create a small triangular opening over a shallow depression where soil had sunk slightly back into the hole dug for that post. She realized it would be possible for her to squirm through. It was the only place the fence was not fastened tight to the ground along there. Just then, she had seen a North Korean soldier on patrol a long way down. He was coming toward her, and she had quickly retreated. Angse was noticeably pregnant then, and several of the woman workers had recalled that in conversations in the last few days.

In these recent days, she had gone several times to check if the fence at that spot would still allow her to squeeze through. Now, on this last day of summer harvesting, Angse thought she knew the complete route they must follow.

After dark when the soldiers on guard at the village could not see her, Angse emptied her last basket with a few vegetables, came out from the trees, and sat on the overturned basket. She nursed again, and changed her baby's diaper. Her baby was almost asleep. Still, she had to speak with her baby; "I'm afraid of what might come now for you Sung, but I must do it. I cannot let you go on to live here and suffer as I have. Anything else, even death as a young child, is better." As she continued talking about her love, Sung's eyes opened for several minutes, she stared up at her mother, then fell asleep.

Rising hesitantly, Angse took a deep breath, and began walking cautiously southward. Her thoughts raced as she clutched the baby in its pouch to her chest. Now came agonizing thoughts of divided loyalties and responsibilities, followed by a sense of great danger. What if authorities on either side caught her?

She walked a few hundred yards until she spied the "Bridge of No Return" area in soft starlight. Hidden in thick shrub cover she repeatedly gazed up and down the fence and saw that no North or South Korean soldiers were just then close to the "Bridge." Quickly, she moved to the place where the fence would yield, knelt down, and pushed the bottom of the fence away and up. She easily shoved the pouch with baby through. Lying as flat as possible she began squirming under the fence. The bottom of the fence grabbed her headscarf, and she shook free. Then it pulled repeatedly at the back of her sweater, but each time she freed herself by wriggling from side to side. Then she crawled until her legs were free and stood up, picked up the baby and rapidly crossed the road. For less than a minute she stood catching her breath. Far down to one side she saw flashlights bouncing as soldiers on patrol were approaching.

Her body trembled as she walked quickly, though uncertainly, along a path she hoped was the one she remembered from a crucial map. The baby awakened and made soft noises. Angse knew they could both now be free if she didn't have to return to care for her young son, husband, their own parents, and two elderly grandparents. Trembling and tense she pressed on.

In five minutes, light from a United Nations Watchtower appeared as she rounded a long curve. She saw the head of a guard in one of the watchtower's windows. Slipping through brush along the path she emerged and softly mounted stairs to a landing at an upper door. She laid the baby down, took a piece of paper from her sweater pocket, and slipped it into the pouch. The baby began to cry. Angse pounded hard twice on the door, and ran down the steps into the brush and waited. A guard came out and picked up the pouch.

"Come see this, there's a little baby here," she shouted in English as she carried the pouch inside. Opening it wider she saw the piece of paper, unfolded it, and exclaimed; "There's a note with this beautiful baby." She read aloud its broken English.

"Sung Je-Aie her name. Pleas care good for her. She need live her life free. Life our place country north not good. She two month five days old. She come from Suragam. I be her mother Angse."

"My God! Suragam is North Korea." The other guard said.

As Angse slipped away she heard all of this coming through the watchtower's open door. She paused once for a few seconds just to hear Sung's louder crying for the last time.

After a few minutes the other guard came down from the tower with a flashlight and searched all around. By this time Angse had rushed back to the "Bridge." A nearly full moon was rising. She hid in low, dense shrubs as two North Korean soldiers marched by along the other side of the fence sweeping areas in all directions with powerful lights. When they had gone far from her she quickly crossed over the road, slithered under the fence, and made her way back, staying inside brush cover so the Kijong-Dong soldiers could not spot her in the now bright moonlight. She reached out and swiftly pulled the basket into her hiding place.

She sat on the basket wondering if she might ever know about Sung's life in years ahead. From her satchel she took an apple she had saved at lunchtime. Stared at it, but could not eat. Thoughts about Sung's future caused her to imagine all sorts of things about a life with freedom and opportunity. Maybe some day she, too, might live free and search for Sung.

But for now she must go home. Then sadness hit hard. Tears filled her eyes, refusing to stop for a long time no matter how often she wiped them away. Sobbing, she stretched out on the ground. Eventually, she fell into fitful sleep.

Dawn was breaking just as Angse heard the bus with its squeaking, grinding brakes. She waited as workers moved onto the fields. Then she emerged and began harvesting.

At dusk, after that long sad day, she boarded the bus, falling asleep for the entire ride home. A few others got off with her at Suragam. None asked about her baby. Angse thought they might be fearful about involvement in anything suspicious or illegal. But two women who had talked to her in the fields were there, and greeted her gently as they walked home. One woman called as they parted: "I hope to see you and baby soon, love to you both."

Back at the Watchtower, within a few hours, two employes of the United Nations Human Rights Agency arrived at the watch tower, and moved Sung, along with Angse's note, to an orphanage in Seoul. After some adjustment, Sung accepted baby formula milk, and grew rapidly. Over the following years she developed into an amazingly bright and curious child. She received excellent education, using the Korean and English languages.

When she was just over five years old she was adopted by a couple from Portland, Oregon. A certificate gave her name, age, place and date of birth, and mother's name. Her adoptive mother was originally from North Korea. She had escaped as a late teenager in 1966, and immigrated to the U.S. She attended the University of California at Berkeley where she met her American husband. After Sung's adoption in 1976, her new parents made certain that Sung continued to use the English and Korean languages.

Sung received college degrees in history, foreign languages, and literature, including a Ph.D. from Portland State. In 2001 she accepted an offer as an assistant professor at Lake Union University. She rented an apartment in the 14th Ward on Freedom Lane, and bought a house there a few years later. She walked a few blocks along Promise Way to the University where she became an outstanding teacher and scholar. She also became an active and devoted participant in that highly unusual 14th Ward community.

Almost every day Angse dreamed of a time when she might begin her search for Sung using information from the orphanage in Seoul.

Charles's First Visit, from Chicago to a New Life, 1972.

Now, we learn about the efforts of realtors to discourage white customers from from choosing houses in the Fourteenth Ward. Charles describes his first experiences.

It was a cool and sunny fall morning as I left the hotel. There were few people on the sidewalk, but plenty of cars passing in both directions. I had walked less than a block when the blare of sirens erupted. Cars swerved to stop at both edges of the street as a red sedan raced past with two police cars in pursuit. Other sirens sprang up nearby as the red sedan veered out of sight around the next corner. In another minute I heard screeching and the sound of the crash. I ran around the corner, and half a block farther on I could see the red car turned half onto its side badly crumpled against the corner of a building. Four police cars were there, and all traffic was being diverted. A policeman waved me back as I came to that corner. The red car was really a mess, and gasoline leaking from it was aflame. It took several more minutes for a fire truck to arrive to extinguish the flames revealing the car as a blackened lump. The siren of the ambulance sang out as it pulled in next to what was once that car. Two policemen ripped open the drivers front door, which was already half open. A medic leaned in holding a mask to his face against the smoke. He backed out shaking his head. I heard him say both of them were dead, and I could see both bodies. They were black men in their twenties or thirties. Then, I heard two of the officers talking.

"Well, that's one way to solve and settle a robbery all in one swoop. This damn part of town is out of control."

"Yes, two bad apples less, and legal and court costs will be minimal."

The second officer walked over to me.

"Did you witness all of this?"

"Not quite. I was on the next street up there, saw the chase, and heard the crash, but I did not see the crashed car and flames until I ran down this block."

"That's as good as an eye witness. I need your name, address and telephone."

"My name is Charles Wilson, but I don't live here. I'm in town for an interview this afternoon."

That's OK, I still need the information, and some identification from you. You will be contacted for a statement, but probably that will be sufficient. What sort of interview?"

"It's with Union Bank for an Assistant Manager job."

"I'm impressed."

As he wrote down information from me I realized for the first time that I was suddenly shaking. The sudden, violent, deaths of two men my age had just hit home.

"Is that all you need from me, officer?"

"Yes, thank you for your cooperation, and good luck at the interview."

As I turned, my gaze fixed for a moment on the blackened wreck causing me to shudder. *"What a waste,"* I thought.

Lost in this feeling of sadness and senselessness I walked slowly back up to the corner, and turned onto the street with my hotel. I noticed the street sign for the first time, it was called Lake Avenue.

Despite haunting feelings about those young deaths my interview went well, and at the end I was told I would be offered the Assistant Manager position in their Monsour branch. I told them this was my third and last interview, and that I would give them an answer in a few days after I talked it over with my wife.

Back at the hotel I called Stella, and told her I was sure the job at Union Bank here was the one I would take, and that I would be in charge of their branch office in some place called

Monsour. And that tomorrow I would call a real estate office, and arrange to look at some neighborhoods and houses. I also wanted to find out where the Monsour Branch was.

As I watched television news that night I learned that the guys who died in that crash had stolen less than a hundred dollars. That the driver had a long record of minor crimes, a ne'er-do-well the announcer commented, but his accomplice had no record. He had been in the army for six years, and was a student in the journalism and writing program at the Community College. He had worked part-time writing articles about local high school sports. Both of them were twenty five, and there was no explanation why the college student was involved other than that the two of them had attended high school together.

Morning came and my appointment with the real estate agent was not until afternoon, so I decided to look around the immediate area. I first walked north of Lake Avenue for several blocks in the area behind the hotel. The houses were fairly old looking, but almost all were large and stately. They were also in good condition for the most part. It was clearly a racially mixed neighborhood. I was impressed by the area, because of the fine houses, though a few were certainly in bad shape, and there were some vacant lots where houses had been removed. Most of the yards and gardens were well kept, but a few were all weeds. I also passed an old high school that was still in excellent shape. Up along the lake front there was a nice area with boat docks and several small stores. I wondered if this was where the robbery had occurred.

From there I walked back along a street named Primrose, and met a woman named Emma working in her front yard. We chatted for quite a while, and from her I learned this was the 14th Ward. Many things she said made it sound like this was a really fine part of the City.

When I got back to Lake Avenue I decided to walk south back to the crash scene. As I walked down that long block, the one I had run down yesterday, I noticed for the first time that there were many nice, and varied, small shops and restaurants with attractive doors and windows, and that the area was clean and tidy, almost to the point of being precious. An interesting contrast to the more conventional area of shops I had just seen up back there to the north on the lake.

When I reached the corner I saw that two white men and a black woman were cleaning the black and brown deposits from the sidewalk and building at the crash site. They had cleaned all of it from the heavy stone work around the corner of the building that had taken the impact. It was built solid, and looked as if it had not been damaged. I crossed over to the front of that building, and was amazed to read the sign over the door: "Union Bank, Monsour Branch." It was truly a beautiful old building and I immediately liked the idea of working in this elegant setting, despite my unpleasant recollections of this place the day before. I told myself that it was just fortuitous that the robbers had swerved down this street and hit my bank in an effort to avoid the police. Then I noticed the irony in the name of this street: "Prospect Street." A promising future prospect for me in this city, and no future for those two.

Back at the Hotel I talked with the Black attendant at the counter.

"What do you think about the residential area behind the hotel, and up along the lake?"

"Excellent area. I have lived there in the 14th Ward for many years. It's a diverse and exciting community.

"One more thing. I need to buy a car. Can you recommend a good place?"

"Yes. One of my neighbors, Jason Harrison, runs the auto store and repair shop on Prospect Street. They have new and used cars of quite a few different makes, U.S. and foreign. Just walk down to Prospect, and go left for two blocks. Everyone trusts that store.

The next day, Charles went there, met Jason Harrison, and bought a car. Jason mentioned that his wife Emma had talked with him at their house the day before.

His encounter with the real estate agent, Susan Borsch was more complex. He tried to suggest looking for a house in the 14th Ward, but she argued, almost vehemently, against it.

"I could show you the only two or three places available there, but I don't recommend it. It's not a desirable neighborhood. A lot of foreigners, black and mexican people. I don't think it's a safe place. Beyond your bank just to the south of the city are many wonderful, reasonably priced, houses I can show you." She does mention the great old house along the lake, where Charles and his wife Stella will move a few years later, buying the house next to Emma and Jason's place.

She takes him to houses in newer suburbs several miles south of Monsour. And that was how he and Stella came to move first to the gated community called South Lawn.

From the restaurant atop the hotel later that day Charles can see that area along the lake. Charles's wife Stella comes from Iowa City, and has a University of Iowa degree in Art, and Art history. She is an excellent painter, and they will soon have two children.

Charles grew up in a suburb of Chicago, and had an unhappy family life. His father was successful, but verbally abusive to his wife, and all four children including Charles— the source of Charles's unusual sensitivity.

A Disturbing Saga Unfolds.

As this part of our story takes place in fall 2003 and early 2004. Jason Jr, usually just called "Junior," is the son of Jason Sr and Emma. Jason Sr first appeared in our story at his father's gas station when he was finishing high school in Detroit in the late 1970s. Jason Jr was born in the Fourteenth Ward in 1981.

Jason Jr. shocks Professor Sung Je-Aie in April 2003 when he stops her in the hallway at the University and says; "I know I should wait to finish my doctoral thesis, but that will take at least two more years. This war in Iraq will be over by then. I owe it to my country to join the army, and serve to make sure Saddam Hussein doesn't get to use those nuclear, biological, or chemical weapons."

"When did you make this decision?"

"Three days ago, when I was in the Library reading the New York Times about our ongoing invasion of Iraq. This is war we have to fight for the Iraqi people, though I certainly don't believe much of what Bush, Cheney, and others in that administration say."

"What do your father and mother say about this?"

"Mom says, flat out, "No, don't do it", and argues it is not a just war, and terrible foreign policy. Dad is confused. He thinks back to how he avoided the draft during the Vietnam War. He has said over and over, "If it was that war, I'd agree with Emma, but I don't know." Still, I can tell he wishes I wasn't going."

Because of his athletic condition, Jason Jr. cruised through the weeks of training, and shipped off to Iraq at the end of July 2003. He was immediately assigned to a guard post at one of the entrances to the large, so-called, Green Zone where the U.S. and Iraq government have many of their offices. On his first day there he saw a beautiful woman dressed in modern, western clothes walk toward their small office building at the post. He asked the soldier standing next to him who she was.

"Her name is Arwa. Isn't she a knockout, what a figure, huh? She's our interpreter, speaks English and Iraqi perfectly. But, she keeps her distance from us soldiers as much as possible. I don't know why."

Arwa was indeed beautiful: long jet black hair, a figure that any model would wish for, large bright, black eyes, a smile of enormous richness, and lovely, fair skin.

When Jason wrote to his parents a week later, telling them of his assignment, they were relieved that he was not in one of the active combat zones they read about almost every day. In that letter he also mentions; "their beautiful interpreter, Arwa Kahlil, who works with him." He said, "I've gotten to know her a bit, though she obviously avoids the other soldiers. Arwa and I get along because she is a graduate student in history and sociology, just like me. So, we have a lot in common to talk about, though not too much about the war. Her few comments about the war make it clear she hates it, and what American forces are doing on many occasions."

Occasionally Arwa mentioned her boyfriend Dawud Hadid, a graduate student in mathematics, but Jason hadn't met him. He suspected they lived together.

Several months passed and Jason Jr. and Arwa became good friends. Jason realized her reason for avoiding, and disliking, the other soldiers was because they frequently called out crude, sexist, things to her as she passed by. Her face turned bright red every time this happened, and staring away she always uttered some sort of unintelligible curse under her breath.

When they were alone after one especially bad occasion when two of the soldiers said things like; "How about we get it together alone tonight, honey?" Jason tried to apologize. She said; "You don't have to apologize. You are civilized. Those jerks are savages, dirt. Their the reason this war is a stupid mistake. Just get them out of here for good. Anyway, I've got to get home and fix dinner. It's my night."

Arwa and Dawud did live together, and had a wonderful, deeply loving, relationship. Their only sad moments came when they talked about the war and what it was doing to their country and people. Each attended a few graduate classes each week at the university, but mostly they worked there on their doctoral dissertations. At the university they saw a few of the tragic effects of the war: fewer classes and students, physical deterioration and dirtier conditions, and above all a sense of fear. At work as a private guard at one of the shops near their apartment, Dawud saw the poor condition of many people on the streets, and twice he had seen the devastation of bombings not far down the street. That evening they talked about the war.

"Dawud, what can we do to end the chaos of this war. Our people, government, and society are coming apart. The poverty and destruction is horrible. Every day civilians, normal citizens are killed by suicide bombers and random firing by both U.S. and Iraqi forces. The Americans never should have come. Our country was none of their business, and the invasion is illegal under International Law."

"I know, I know Arwa. At times I feel desperate to find a way to do something. I hate the Americans so much that I sometimes think suicide bombing is the only recourse I have."

"Don't say that. We have each other, and our university work. We'll make a good life together after the war."

"How? Make a good life? What life? There will be nothing left, if it ever ends. The destruction will go on and on. We'll get old and eventually live in poverty once the Americans leave. Our country will be ruined for centuries by cultural strife and fighting beyond our lifetimes. Better to end it now and take as many of the Americans with us as possible. And that will ..."

Dawud was interrupted by two nearby explosions.

"See like that. That will be my best answer to the Americans."

Tears flooded down Arwa's cheeks. "No, No. That's not the answer. The only time I have thoughts like that is when one of those idiot soldiers says something sexist and ugly to me at work. I hate them all. No, not all, Jason is different. He thinks the war is wrong, and wishes he had never joined. He is a good friend and I want you to meet him someday."

Eventually, they ate the supper that had grown cold, and turned to class work for tomorrow at the university. Though, both had trouble concentrating, and eventually went early to bed. The next day, December 13, 2003, Saddam Hussein, ousted President, was captured near Tikrit.

As two more months passed the situation all around them in Baghdad got worse. To make Arwa's life worse, three of the soldiers had repeatedly grabbed her or patted her on her back or behind. Jason had tried to stop this, but they continued do it whenever he was not on duty. And because of his criticisms of their behavior the other soldiers treated him badly. This doubled Arwa's hatred toward them.

On a Friday after a particularly bloody day of fighting in Baghdad, Arwa rushed home to start supper, narrowly missing a firefight only a block away from their apartment. She was relieved when Dawud arrived.

"That smells good Arwa. What is it?"

"Rice, fish bits, and corn. I've made it a hundred times, but the sauce is a little spicier this time. I was worried about you when I heard those explosions."

"Why?"

"Because you talked about being a suicide bomber."

"Oh that. Don't worry. I may do it, but I'm not ready yet. I did think hard about it today when Ali told me his brother had done it at a police station killing three Americans and six Iraqi officers. That was a bad choice. The goal is to kill Americans, not our own people."

"I wish you wouldn't talk about it, Dawud."

"I know it upsets you, but do you realize that is the fourth of my childhood friends who's done it."

"Is it that many? I just remember when Ada did it, she was a good friend for both of us."

"Yeah. Lets talk about something else."

As Dawud walked to his little desk, Arwa thought how handsome he was with a strong build, small mustache, short hair, and smooth skin—even with so much stress that might otherwise wrinkle his face.

The next day was very bad for Dawud. Three university students he knew were killed by American gunfire, and the wife and child of a longtime friend were killed by Americans in another firefight.

The same day was especially difficult for Arwa. As soon as Jason went off duty shortly after she arrived two of the guards made their usual nasty cracks several times when she went out to question Iraqis coming to enter the Green Zone. Once as she had walked back toward the office one soldier called out; "You do have a sweet fanny, girl."

The worst part of the next day came as she was eating supper alone because Dawud was working late in the library at the university. She could not stop thinking about suicide bombing.

She thought: *I think that Dawud is getting closer to doing it. The killings yesterday hit him harder than anything previously. For me the primitive Americans like that idiot calling out about my fanny in public is not enough. But it certainly makes me hate almost all of them. It's really the terrible killing the Americans are doing that makes me want to kill them. Jason is the rare exception. We had a great talk this morning about medieval history and modern Iraq's origin. But those other soldiers are eager to kill us. Over and over again, I've heard them say they wish they would be assigned to a combat unit so they can take out some of the stupid Iraqis. They would kill women and children. Like what happened last week to the whole family that lived in the house next to my parents. Wife and three children killed by "mistake" in a full scale attack on their house, while the father was at his shop in Sadr City. It could have been my mom and my brother Saied. Maybe we have to fight back the only way we can.*

She washed dishes and turned to her studies, but it was not enough to suppress her terrible thoughts; *Maybe it is the only way for us.*

Several weeks later she came home as Dawud was making dinner. She saw a large backpack on one of the chairs.

"What do you have in that huge backpack, Dawud?"

"Never mind for now. We'll talk about it later, after dinner."

After supper when he finished washing the dishes, he opened the backpack, and showed her the incredible bomb materials, and how simply it all went together. She burst into tears, rushed to bed and did not emerge all night. Dawud put the backpack with bombs in the back of a closet. Later he told her it came from a group called "Organized Against Americans."

Coming home two weeks later, Arwa saw a scrap of plastic on the kitchen floor. There were several other pieces of plastic and paper, and some elastic tape on the table. She knew instantly what they were, and rushed to the closet. An explosive vest was missing along with other stuff. She steeled herself when a knock on the door came two minutes later. She did not cry as a student she knew from the university said; "Dawud did it big time. He killed at least ten American soldiers standing around the remains of a vehicle with three dead Americans that had been bombed minutes before. We will remember and always celebrate his courage."

She thanked him. After he left she cried for a long time. Finally, still crying, she called her parents and told them about Dawud's death. They were shocked. Her mom said she could sort of understand it, but hated the thought that any person so young would feel compelled to sacrifice himself. After a short conversation about other things Arwa stopped crying, and they ended with promises to get together soon.

Still, in a horribly complex, contorted, way, Arwa knew her turn might come. I realize now that Dawud had really departed inside himself and from me a month or two ago. I couldn't understand why he no longer wanted sex, and why he spoke so briefly much of the time. Yet I could tell when he held me in bed, and at other times, that he loved me as deeply as ever. It was strange. As days passed he was there and not there at the same time. His mind and body sometimes seemed often to be elsewhere. *Now, I feel some of the same things he mentioned earlier. That somehow personal sacrifice, his and mine, can change things. Before now we never thought at these young ages that choosing a short life could be meaningful. I see there just might be this one way to let many much younger Iraqis have their whole lives to live, to not be slaughtered by the bombs and the Americans. A chance, too, for our country to be peaceful some day. A day that will come sooner because we, Dawud and I, and many others, choose to show the Americans that they can't take our lives, and our country, and our leader Saddam, despite all his flaws, and many wrong actions. That we chose to kill them in the cause of peace is simple logic after all.*

Days passed and Arwa's thoughts about suicide bombing came only briefly, though she knew another bomb was in the backpack, and sometimes thought of that. Early one evening as she was leaving the university the student that had come to tell her of Dawud's suicide stopped to ask if she would like to join a few students gathering to briefly honor Dawud. When she entered the room she was surprised to see more than thirty students from many departments. One by one each of them recalled how great a friend he had been, including specific recollections about his generosity, brilliance, humor, and deep concerns about the war, and the country's future.

The last to speak was the student that had come to her door. He said; "Dawud's was a great sacrifice. If a few thousands of Iraqis do as he did, it will mean tens of thousands of American soldiers killed and many more seriously wounded. The Americans will give up and leave. We will have banished them, and left a better world for the young people and students to come." Arwa nodded politely toward all of them as she left without saying anything.

Two evenings later a call came from her father. His youngest brother, a shopkeeper, his wife and their three young children had been gunned down in their house by American soldiers in Falluja. Her father said: "I got a call from another friend in Falluja. The soldiers broke into my brother's house at night when they were sleeping in search of Iraqis who planted a roadside bomb that earlier killed three of their soldiers. They were breaking into house after house killing innocent people. What are we going to do?"

When she hung up the phone Arwa felt like she was in a trance, her thoughts drifting wildly backward and forward in time. Finally, she shook her head hard and cried aloud; "I'll follow Dawud, the Dawud I love so much."

After a long time watching people, many with children, passing by the window, Arwa thought of her parents, and how she could tell them about Dawud's sacrifice, and her plan. I can't face them, but I want them to understand.

In her early college years Arwa had taken literature and writing courses. She had written poetry frequently, and she suddenly realized she could tell her parents with a poem. She went to the table and started writing. To her surprise it came easily.

> Dawud, my love, went solemnly to his end,
> Only just a few short days ago.

It was a deeply thought out choice.
For him a necessity driven by the evil,
Laid on our Country by Americans.
Still, I think he found calm resolve,
Maybe even a welcome happiness,
Mixed with his solemnity.
I love him with all I have.
I must quickly follow him,
Though I have no idea,
Whether he and I will meet again.

I know for certain, deep inside,
That I, too, must fight this evil,
With all I have, my life. And,
Hopes for many better lives to come.
And peace yet for you, Mom and Dad.
Above all, a happier life for Saied,
And many more of our Country's children.
My love for you is great, eternal.

She folded the page, slipped it into an envelope, addressed it, and walked out and mailed it. When she got back she started sorting through some traditional, Muslim clothing she had not used for years. She found her hijab veil and her long, black abayah cloak. Laying them on the bed she stood for a long time staring at them. Then, she went to the closet and pulled out Dawud's backpack. She found the bomb to strap around her waist, and the switch to detonate it. She carefully read the attached instructions. Then, she removed a smaller object and realized it was another bomb with a timer and directions for its use. Her thoughts raced as she realized she could use both of them.

At dawn, with just the two other guards with him, Jason opened the letter from Sung that had arrived. Included were letters from both his parents. He could tell all of them were deeply concerned about his safety, because the war was going badly, and the justifications for it had evaporated. His father wrote: "I look forward to talking with you about your future role in this war when you get your first chance to come for a brief visit on leave." He knew his dad was thinking about how he might avoid having to return at all, but wouldn't bring that up knowing that such letters were monitored. It was clear it had been opened and resealed. He wrote back to tell them he was all right. He again mentioned the woman Arwa and their interesting exchanges, concluding that she dislikes this war as much as we do.

Their other interpreter came out of the office about ten minutes before noon and said;" I have to rush off to a doctor's appointment. Arwa will be here any minute."

Jason finished guard duty right at noon, having started at three that morning. Three soldiers arrived for their guard duty as he signed out in the office. The two soldiers that had been on duty with him stayed to talk with the new guys. All five of them were shocked when Arwa walked up dressed in a full length abayah and the hijab. One of them laughed loudly and said; "What is this? The real Arwa, hiding her sexy self. What are you afraid of cutie?"

Arwa ignored him and went into the office. Junior was surprised to see her in such garb, but said nothing. He simply said he was on his way to get some sleep. After a brief conversation with her they walked out of the office together. She watched him go around the building onto the path headed to the barracks, and waited to be sure he would be safe, and thought: *Since Dawud died I have come to love Jason, too, and I know he feels like that about me. He recently mentionedI that maybe in a year when he goes home I might go with him to America. He said people there would not treat me the way some of these stupid American soldiers do. I wish we could have gone on to live together someday in America. But it will not be, I have to fight to defend my own people and country, just as Dawud did.*

Another soldier said to her; "Ah, you're back sweet, sexy honey. What you got in that bag, a present for us? What can I do for you?"

"Not a thing, thank you," Arwa said sarcastically in a loud voice as she stared defiantly at him for a minute. Then, she walked around the far side of the building and carefully set five minutes on the timer with the small bomb. She laid the plastic bag with the bomb against the front of the office, and walked swiftly past the soldiers and down the street. One of of the soldiers shouted; "You forgot your bag sassy woman."

Half way to the barracks, Jason had realized he'd left a book he was reading in the office, turned, and rapidly walked back. He rounded the corner of the office building as the bomb exploded. All five soldiers were killed instantly, and Jason lay dying in a pool of his own blood, a bloody leg from one of the soldiers lying across his body. Blood and body parts were everywhere. The front windows and door of the office were blown in. The worker inside was slightly wounded, and when he came out he saw plastic shreds from Arwa's bag, realized she was gone, and had done this intentionally. He walked over to Jason, and heard his last utterance; "Where's Arwa?" That worker's report to his commander sent shock waves through the entire Green Zone security ranks. "None of us are safe, they really hate us. How can we even trust our thoroughly checked interpreters," the commander wrote at the end of his report.

Arwa's main plan was focused on a major road block that always had a dozen or more soldiers and police on guard, With some usually just standing around talking. It was a two mile walk down the street to that post and she walked slowly. She heard the blast behind her, and instantly her lips and face were gripped in an awful grimace. Her shoulders shook uncontrollably as she moved on. She occasionally paused to look in shop windows, as if she was shopping, her effort to avoid attention. Breathing deeply again and again she calmed down. As she approached the road block she saw quite a few American soldiers and one Iraqi policeman. She walked quietly up to the police officer.

"Show me your ID mam." he said.

She swiftly brushed by him to get closer to the crowd of soldiers, and detonated her bomb. Fourteen American soldiers and the police officer died instantly as Arwa's body was blown apart in the tremendous explosion.

A local Bagdad paper and television station reported this suicide, and an earlier bombing at a Green Zone entrance. The paper's report said the second was done by a woman suicide bomber, and that it was no longer unusual for woman to do this. They thought the bombing at the Green Zone was also the work of a woman, because two people down the road there saw a woman walk quickly away from there a minute or two before the large explosion killed two guards and one other man.

A police hunt for Arwa turned up nothing after they searched her apartment and later questioned her parents. They did find the empty backpack lying on the kitchen floor in Arwa's apartment, but all else there was clean and in order. They never linked her to either of the bombings. Especially the latter one, because her remains were nothing but a lot of little charred bits.

Barton, a wealthy man, comes to Lake Union City, and eventually the 14th Ward, contrary to efforts by a real estate agent.

In 2009, Barton Waterson Sampson looked pensively at the panorama of tall buildings in Minneapolis stretching away from the windows of his top floor office. It was his last day. During his career here he had been the CEO at different times of three independent corporations, all of which were highly successful under his leadership. Tomorrow he will be fully retired, no longer associated in any way with Big Stores Corporation. He walked over and looked at himself in the gold framed mirror on the far wall, thinking: *Here I am. Sixty-eight years old. Hair almost completely gray, and balding from the front, A few long lines in my face. I'm in pretty good shape physically, just a little overweight. It's been a good life here, and it made me wealthy. It is time for something different.*

He had longed to move from Minneapolis for several years—to find a new and somewhat quieter place. A year ago he read in a magazine about a place called Lake Union City; somewhat smaller, but quite sophisticated in many ways. After a number of extensive trips to at least two dozen cities and towns, he decided Lake Union City was his choice. This morning he had called a real estate agent there, and bought an airline ticket for an evening flight. He'll meet the agent tomorrow. With a sigh, he picked up his briefcase and walked out to talk with his secretary of many years.

"Well, as you know, Julia, I'll be gone. I just want to say I'll miss you. It has been wonderful working with you in two different companies."

"Will you still be around town for a little while, Barton?"

"No. This evening I fly to the place called Lake Union City that I've mentioned a few times. My house here is sold, and I'll buy a house there. I've arranged to have all my stuff moved when I call for it, even sold my car. I hope you will come to visit after I'm settled there. Promise?"

"I will come on one of my vacations. Maybe I'll like the place so much I'll move there when I retire in two years. Who knows? As a satisfied divorcee, I'll have all the freedom, too. And I'm grateful to you for the opportunities you've made possible for me over the last two decades."

"No thanks needed. You have been amazing in helping me to keep my head on straight through some really rough political and economic times. Not to mention all the darn board meetings you helped with. Now, I'll just say goodbye, and walk out with nothing but my briefcase."

She stood, came around her desk, hugged him, and kissed him on the lips. "I will miss you, Barton."

He hugged her tightly and said; "Thank you. That makes my departure really special. I'll write you about how life goes in Lake Union City."

At the door he turned and waved, and saw a few small tears at the corners of her eyes, and thought; *A very smart woman with a still beautiful face and body, Damn good for a middle aged woman. He smiled again and was gone.*

Barton and the real estate agent looked at a dozen or more houses for sale, All were in the million-dollar range. The agent claimed these were in the best neighborhoods in the city, but in fact Barton didn't really see much of the city. The houses he saw were all in an area on the far east side of the city where many affluent people lived. He bought a large house in that neighborhood for just under a million dollars. Over the next few months he met some neighbors, but realized soon that they mostly kept to themselves. It was not a very social community, and that disappointed him.

Over the coming year Barton explored a lot more of the city. He was most fascinated by an area right along the lake on the west side. He thought it was interesting, because it involved people who appeared to be of many different origins all mixed together: African-Americans, Asians, Hispanics, Caucasians, and many that had Middle Eastern names. Houses and yards were in very good shape in that neighborhood. He especially liked walking down the long curving stretch of Primrose Street with houses on one side, and a long, wide stretch of park along the beautiful lake on the other side. He saw houses that were as large as the one he had bought. Many lovely houses also stood on the adjacent side streets. He found out this part of the City was the Fourteenth Ward, and he had no trouble realizing that his real estate agent was a big time racist. On one walk along Primrose Street he watched the happy faces, and heard wonderful music, in a large community gathering.

Thinking he might eventually move over there he went back fairly frequently to explore. Often, people living there stopped to chat with him, and occasionally invited him to their houses or onto a deck or porch for tea or coffee. On warm summer days he liked to watch parents and children swimming in the lake, or paddling about in canoes or kayaks. The lakeshore was open to all residents, though there were no docks. The people just carried their boats to the water from their homes or off the tops of cars. There was a public boatyard far up where Primrose reached an area with well maintained stores or shops, and a few restaurants.

He took longer walks in the Ward; down Primrose, over Freedom Lane, to Lake Avenue, and then down South Street with all the lovely Middle Eastern style shops and restaurants, (and a few years later with one new, large, elegant "Chinese/ Japanese" restaurant.) He often went farther east or west when he reached Prospect Street. He learned that whole area called the Monsour district was also part of the Fourteenth Ward.

During his first year there, on several occasions, Barton's daughter Maria with her two small children, Wallace and Marty, and her husband Lin Yang came to visit. These were times of great pleasure for Barton. He had been lonely in his last years in Minneapolis. His wife Clara had died three years before he left. He loved Maria's two, strikingly beautiful, young children, and thought her husband Lin, a rising engineer, was an excellent, loving father for them, and a delightful, highly intelligent fellow to talk with. Maria and Lin had bought a house in Cleveland, Ohio, and Maria had been a stay-at-home mom for the last five years. Before that she was a history teacher in a local high school.

Then, early one morning, three months into his second year, Barton received the shocking phone call. It was Maria. He could tell by her sobbing and halting speech, that she was terribly upset.

"Oh Dad, Lin was k-killed in an accident on his way to w-work. His car was h-hit by a huge semi truck an hour ago. They s-said he d-died instantly.

For several minutes she couldn't talk again through her crying.

"Don't try to talk until you can quiet down. Just take your time," Barton said.

Finally she calmed down a little. "Dad I don't know what to do. There's too much to do now." she sobbed.

"Oh my God, this is terrible Maria. Can I come down there and help you?"

"Yes. Come Dad. I need you. I'm desperate. Just to have you here will make a difference."

"I'll leave immediately, and will be there by late evening. Just rest and spend all your time with Wallace and Marty. I love you Maria. I'll be there."

"I love you Dad. thank you for coming."

"Goodbye dear. I'm on my way."

"Good bye Dad."

Barton drove to Cleveland. For several days he and Maria just took time to adjust to the shock of Lin's death, and mostly spent time with the children, other than to arrange Lin's funeral. They notified Lin's parents in China, but it was impossible for them to make the trip even if Lin's funeral was delayed. Lin's funeral was four days later on Monday morning. A large crowd of friends and coworkers gathered for the ceremony and reception. Afterward, Barton and Maria held each other and the children as Lin's body was taken away for cremation. The next day they rested, and took long walks with the children.

Wednesday morning opened with bight sunlight. After breakfast Barton sat at the table with Maria, and helped her plan how they might deal with the house, and the funeral expenses. He proposed that she come to Lake Union City to live a little while with him. He had plenty of room. She could figure out where she wanted to live. She might look for a job in Lake Union City, or somewhere else. Somehow she would find a way to start a new life.

There was a sizable mortgage on the house Lin and Maria had bought, and because she had been a stay-at-home mom these last few years Maria would have no way to keep up with the mortgage payments. Barton said he could settle that, and put the little money recouped into her savings account. The next day at the bank Barton arranged to pay off the mortgage. Over the next two days they packed. Then they drove to Lake Union City. It was early June.

The children were pretty close to ages when they would start school. Wallace was four years old, and had been in preschool, Marty was three and would start preschool the next fall. After a few weeks of settling down, Barton and Maria began exploring the schools of Lake Union City. It did not take long before they found out that the finest schools were in the Fourteenth Ward—the very area on the west side by the lake where Barton had admired some of the larger houses along Primrose Street and on adjoining side streets.

The quality of the schools was in part the result of a very active community organization that had been in operation for years, and in part because of a very close relationship with Lake Union University, which was right in the area with the elementary, middle and high schools on Forsyth Street. They learned that one of the professors there, named Sung Je-Aie, was also closely associated with the development of the schools. At a meeting with her they learned a great deal about how the schools in that Ward achieved their outstanding results. She also showed them extensive ratings from both local and national studies that concluded the Fourteenth Ward schools were truly superior, the best in the City, with high national ratings. She also brought out independent comparisons that showed they were far better than either of the two charter schools in town, or any of the surrounding suburban schools.

The day after meeting with Sung, Barton called his real estate agent. He asked about houses available in the Fourteenth ward, possibly on Primrose street.

"Oh, you don't want to live there!, I'm surprised." were the agent's first words.

"Why surprised," said Barton. "I'm particularly interested in the area because of its high quality schools."

"I guess the schools are OK, but the neighborhood is a complex mixture of races, and incomes, and cultural backgrounds—quite a few blacks. The most expensive houses are no more than five hundred thousand."

"Are there any on Primrose for sale?"

"Let me look. Yes, there are two. They're large and expensive. Probably why they haven't moved in over six months."

"My daughter and I want to see them tomorrow, if possible."

"Ok. If you insist, but I can't understand why. Is it all right if I pick you up at ten in the morning?"

"That will be fine."

The second house they visited was every bit as large as Barton's east side house, and cost half as much. It was in beautiful condition with a large yard with many flowering gardens, and beautiful front shrubbery along Primrose Street. It had lovely views of the lake from front windows on three floors. The children ran and climbed all over the place, inside and out, while Barton conferred with Maria. Both ended up shaking their heads yes. As they walked out Barton turned to the agent, William Concourse.

"We will take this house. I'll come to your office after we drop off Maria and the children, and I'll put down whatever amount of money is needed to seal the deal. After that my house can go on the market as soon as possible."

"OK. If you're sure. I don't think I've ever sold a house over here before."

That evening Barton and Maria and the kids went back to look at the house, and its surroundings. Several neighbors stopped to talk with them, and offered welcoming greetings. Among them was Charles Wilson and his wife Stella who lived next door to the house Barton was buying. When Barton mentioned his realtor's name Charles told about how the same guy had talked him into buying in a suburb, saying 'you don't want to live there' when Charles asked about Fourteenth Ward houses near the lake.

Two months later Barton's house sold, and the move to Primrose Street was complete. Nothing was more fun for all four of them in their early days there than walking all over the neighborhood, and visiting the schools, boatyard, University, and shops. On one occasion they met with Sung at the University. She was delighted they had come to the Ward.

Over the next two years they met many more neighbors and participated in numerous activities with the Community Association. The schools for Wallace and Marty proved to be excellent. The community was incredibly active, exciting and joyful.

Over these years Barton had frequently written to Julia Louise Clark, his former secretary. She had visited four times over the years, and their fondness for each other had grown stronger with each visit.

That evening after the Community Gathering he wrote an impassioned letter about the impending schools fight and his plan to join it. He also invited her to visit again. Two weeks later she wrote; "I've just retired and I can visit anytime." Barton picked her up at the airport a month later.

At the same time the great influx of children from Central America was well underway. A few children came with one parent, and others arrived alone and found a relative. When a center for these immigrants was established in an empty warehouse in the Ward it never filled because the children, with or without a parent, were "adopted" into families in the Ward. This Latino diversity further enriched the already amazing schools. Barton and his wife Maria adopted two of these children, a boy and a girl named Carlos and Ana. Both were fifteen years old, and two years later they were students in one of Sung's World History classes at the University. The nationally and ethnically wider immigration waves followed, and the Ward helped many of those as well.

It was many years after Arwa's suicide bombing and Jason Jr's death, before most people in the Ward learned the full story about Emma's travail.

Emma's agonizing experience started when she learned of Junior's death in Iraq. Here is the best record of Emma's suffering and recovery.

Emma heard knocking on the door of their house in Lake Union City. When she opened it There were two American military officers, one woman and one man.

"May we come in, please," the woman said. "We have some bad news for you."

Emma turned and called out to Jason Sr; "Come at once."

Emma almost fainted on the couch as they told of Junior's death. Jason stood silently as they explained when and how he died, but without any specific details other than the date, and that it was a bombing. Tears came to Jason's eyes. After a short discussion, the female officer handed Emma a packet of Junior's belongings found where he had lived in the barracks. She could hardly let herself look at Jason and Emma, as both of them were crying. The officers apologized and departed.

Many days later when Emma first sorted through Junior's items returned by the military officers she found her, Jason's, and Sung's letters, Junior's camera, and many photographs of people and surroundings in Baghdad. One of the photographs was of Jason standing with an amazingly beautiful woman wearing modern clothes. Written at the bottom of it was "me and my wonderful friend, Arwa Kahlil."

The next evening before supper when he came in from the yard and found Emma filling her glass a second time with a large amount of bourbon, Jason was shocked.

"Emma! I've never seen you drink that stuff! I thought you didn't like it."

"I really don't, but I need something to settle my nerves. I spent much of the day looking at all the things we have in photos, letters, and everything else we've saved during Junior's life until now. It hit hard and ..." She stopped talking as tears welled up and ran done her cheeks. He could see she had been crying a lot. In truth, he, too, had cried quite a bit that day. He wrapped her in his arms, holding tight.

"Drinking won't mend us. It won't bring our boy back. Now, we still have each other, Lorita, and all our friends. We'll make it if we keep strong together."

He failed to calm her. Sobbing she squirmed free and reached for her bourbon glass, drank more, and filled it again as she moved to a comfortable chair in the living room, where after another hour more than half of her glass of bourbon was gone as she fell into a drunken sleep. Later Jason had to help her to bed, and she slept until late morning the next day. It was only the beginning of Emma's resort to her chosen "alcohol therapy."

Late the next afternoon she went to the nearby liqueur store, coming home with an assortment of a few wines, and numerous hard liqueurs. Though even more surprised, Jason yielded when she suggested that they share drinks, thinking that it would probably do both of them some good. It became a nightly custom, but during the following days Emma would sneak additional alcohol whenever Jason was away.

She frequently thought; The pain from Junior's death is too great. I need this escape. It's making my life possible. I'll control it."

"You are not controlling your drinking when most nights I have to put you to bed." Jason declared one day.

Emma's excessive drinking continued unabated for three weeks. On the last day of those three weeks Jason had a busy day, and a long dinner meeting. Earlier on that day Emma started drinking whiskey in early afternoon, and continued into the evening with no food. She then carried a bottle of whiskey with her onto the porch, and continued sipping it as she sat there in the gathering dusk. Fortunately, she had turned on the porch light an hour early, because an hour later she saw a neighbor Margaret Taylor walking her dog, and tried to step off the porch to greet her. She fell forward onto the flagstone walk hitting her head hard. The neighbor saw this and called out; "Are you all right Emma?" No answer. She walked over and looked at Emma. The side of her forehead was bleeding. She lay half on the walkway with one leg curled around a small shrub Jason had planted beside the walkway a week earlier. Margaret's repeated calls made it clear Emma was unconscious. Margaret pulled her cellphone from her pocket and dialed 911. Within ten minute an ambulance swept in, and after examining the still silent Emma, they put her on a stretcher and slid her into the ambulance. With the siren roaring the ambulance raced to the hospital. Margaret waited to tell Jason what had happened when he arrived twenty five minutes later.

Jason was shaken when Margaret related what had happened to Emma. He called Lorita, and they agreed to meet at the hospital at once. Emma was still unconscious when Lorita left the hospital a few hours later. Emma awakened three hours later as Jason tried unsuccessfully to talk with her. Nurses checked on Emma frequently. Lorita arrived back at five the next morning. An hour later a doctor came in, just as Jason arrived.

"Good morning. I'm Doctor Williamson. I was here last night when they brought Mrs. Richardson in. The good news I have is that she will recover completely. The bad news is that her blood alcohol level last night was extremely high. One of the nurses who checked on her during the night reported she was still really drunk once she woke up. Did you observe that as well, Sir?"

"Yes." Jason replied. "Ever since our son was killed in Iraq she has been drinking heavily every day, something she never did before."

"How long has this been going on?"

"For about two months doctor."

"Knowing this, I can't recommend that she go home. Although, of course, she will be released today, and can go home. But, I recommend we reassign her to the alcohol and drug treatment clinic here in the hospital. They will work hard to give her control over her drinking. Their nurses, psychologists, and a psychiatrist, have excellent records of success. Does that sound like a good idea?"

Both Lorita and Jason nodded yes immediately.

And so it was that Emma went into two months of treatment. She stayed in a sort of dorm room with two other women. A fourth bed and desk were unoccupied. Her first week was pure misery, and she did as little as the routine of twice daily meetings required. She slept a lot. Several times in the first two weeks, misery with an intense sense of shame made her think about suicide. It was almost as difficult a time for her over several more weeks as she kept the recommended diary each day. All her agony over Junior's death was still there, but she increasingly became determined to never again seek escape with alcohol.

The first two weeks of Emma's treatment were very difficult for Lorita, Jason, Sung, Charles, Stella, Barton Sampson, and a few other friends. At least two or three of them came for a short stay with Emma each day, and they definitely helped with her recovery.

Twice daily sessions with a small group of recovering patients, all women, and the woman psychologist, were also agonizing at first. Emma could not talk at all until the third week. Then little by little she let out her story and pain, crying as she did. The others were patient, and several of them expressed equal suffering. By the fourth week they were all calmer, and at times related happier recollections. Emma knew by this time she was regaining control over her grief. She knew she could face Junior's death without thought of alcohol. One essential feature of her recovery was her therapist urging her to cry as often as necessary while she thought of all the wonderful experiences she had shared with Junior—seeking especially memories that made her suddenly smile or laugh, and wanting to share those memories soon with her husband and daughter.

By the fourth week she had started spending a lot of time reading in their small library with abundant books, magazines, and the daily newspaper. She always sat near the large window facing westward from that fifth floor. It brought her peace as she stared at beautiful Lake Union quite far away. It reminded her of their house by the Lake on Primrose Street, and she began longing to be home, a feeling that grew stronger each day. She also now used some of the equipment in their small exercise room each day. Her dairy entries grew longer, and increasingly laid out plans for her future activities.

Then the eight weeks were over. Jason came to take her home. She was still a little shaky, especially as they drove up their driveway. She got out, walked to the porch, and stopped, staring at the chair she had been in just before her fall.

"I don't remember any of it after I saw Margaret with her dog out there on the street," she said, as Jason came up beside her, and curled his arm around her shoulders.

"Maybe it's best if you don't have to remember. It's behind us now, and we have good lives to live. Let's go on in."

They climbed the steps onto the porch. Emma stopped, stared again at the chair, and turned to look at the steps. Shaking her head side to side she followed Jason inside, and immediately went to open the cabinet where she kept her liquor. With one glance at the bottles she cried out. "Never again!" Jason hugged and kissed her for several minutes.

Later that day Lorita came, and was soon followed by a dozen friends and neighbors. Over the following days her closest friends came to visit. In a week she knew she was almost well again. She could stand the pain even when she went to look again at the few of Junior's things the officers had brought from Iraq. When she stared again at the photograph of Junior and Arwa she said to herself; "I'd like to meet Arwa some day. She may have been the first and only young woman he had yet come to love. She is so beautiful. Perhaps we can travel to Iraq and meet her."

Emma could now even bring herself to show that picture of Junior and Arwa to some of her closest friends. On rare occasions she would even have a glass of wine with Jason or friends. It was proof of her cure, because any thought of hard liquor now made her feel ill.

She soon went back to her usual Fourteenth Ward committee meetings and became involved with two major issues: the struggle to accept a new, additional, non Middle Eastern restaurant on South Street in the Monsour area. And then a vicious battle to keep all the excellent 14th Ward schools just as they are, despite the fact that the School Board planned to close all of them, relocate all the teachers, and bus all the students to other schools in Lake Union City. Barton Sampson was a frequent visitor after her return home. Through him and Sung she learned all about the big, ongoing, school fight. Their reports shocked her. Though it would be several weeks before she took seriously the suggestion from Barton, and others, that she run for election to the School Board herself as part of that fight, and she did run.

She also joined downtown and airport protests against the Iraq War once or twice each week. Beyond her loss of Junior, she now saw that the Bush/Cheney War would be a terrible disaster for millions of people—as the years to come would make ever clearer. Unfortunately, the protests increasingly became scenes of protest and counter protest, with the worst cursing and name calling Emma had experienced. She had never before been a "fucking bitch," more that once. In many other ways she came to realize that this irrational war was tearing City and Country apart. Some of her saddest moments came when previously wounded soldiers, missing legs and arms, joined the protests, only to also be called ugly names by a few pro-war people. Driving home with Lorita after one particularly vicious counter-protest Lorita sighed, and spoke so softly that Emma, who was driving, could hardly hear her; "Is there really any reason, any hope, left."

Still, the much more peaceful Fourteenth Ward had become a retreat to liberal sanity for its residents and businesses. It was 2008 and Barak Obama had been elected President.

A Rescue, 2008.

When she walked out of the high school with another member of the Fourteenth Ward Council, Emma was surprised to see how hard it was snowing. Two hours earlier it had been slick with ice on the roads, but there had been little snow. Now, it appeared there was about three inches.

"Amazing," she said. "We've only been at Council meeting for about two hours, maybe a little more. It's going to be tricky driving home because I know there's ice underneath all this snow. We both need to be careful."

"You're right, Emma. Give me a call when you get home just so we can both check that we made it."

"Okay Marsha, I'll call you."

Even as she steered the car out of the parking lot, Emma could tell that it was slippery. She drove carefully over the two and a half miles from the high school to her house on Primrose Street. As she turned into her driveway the car slid sideways. Boy, this driveway is really slippery, she thought.

When she entered the house she saw Jason at his computer in the den.

"It is really getting nasty out there, Jason. There's ice underneath quite a lot of snow now, and my car slid around a lot just on that short drive from the high school. I almost lost the car on our driveway."

"Yes, I looked out the window just a few minutes ago, and saw the snow is piling up. I've got to go out and shovel, otherwise I might not be able to make it to work tomorrow. And I have to get to work tomorrow. Some of my dealerships are in pretty good shape, but others are not doing well at all. The one at Mansour, where my office is, has had good sales recently, but other dealers are in big trouble with this recession. So, here I go a shoveling."

"Oh, I don't want you to. That driveway is so slick you might fall and injure yourself. It's really cold out there, too. The radio said its already two below zero."

"I'll be very careful, but I've got to get the shoveling done. I'm sure I'll have to shovel at least once more before I leave in the morning. I'll put some salt down as I shovel."

After shoveling the snow for almost an hour, Jason watched his neighbor Charles driving into his driveway next door. He knew from an earlier conversation that Charles feared he was going to face a very difficult meeting earlier this night. Like many of his car dealerships, Jason knew a lot of branch banks in the Lake Union Bank system were in trouble, including Charles's Mansour Bank.

Must have been a difficult meeting, because I saw him leave around six and now it's past eleven; Jason thought.

Jason continued watching as Charles drove his car to the back end of his driveway, and parked in about a foot of heavy snow. His wife Stella's car was in one part of the garage, and the other part was still full of boxes from their move here two months ago.

Jason had known Charles for quite a while, and even sold him that car a few years ago when he first arrived, when he lived at first in one of the suburbs, and became manager of the Mansour branch bank. From lots of financial dealings, including numerous car loans, he knew that the Mansour branch was in fairly good shape, partly due to his very talented Assistant Manager, Bertha Green. Sadly, Bertha had been the single mother of the young college student, Leroy, who died as a passenger in that car that crashed against the Mansour bank a few years ago.

Jason saw Charles get out of his car and take one step. Suddenly, his feet flew forward out from under him, and he fell backward banging his head hard on the driver's window. He slumped to the ground on his back, and made no move to get up.

"Charles! Charles!" Jason yield. "Oh my God! He's knocked out, He'll freeze to death. I've got to get him inside."

Jason pushed his way through dense shrubbery on the side of Charles's yard, and rushed across the yard. He grabbed Charles under his armpits, wheeled him around, and dragged him to the front door. Holding him up with one arm he frantically pushed the doorbell, and pounded hard on the door. Stella opened the door, and was shocked to watch Jason dragging her husband through the door and hallway into the living room, where he laid him on a sofa.

"What's happened, Jason?"

"When he got out of his car, he took one step fell backwards hitting his head against the car, and just laid there. He hit his head very hard, because I heard a loud crack when he hit it. We've got to call for an ambulance right away. Let me make the call, please?"

"Yes, please do. I'm starting to shake."

Jason walked into the next room, picked up the phone and dialed 911. He told the operator that they desperately needed an ambulance to take a man to emergency with what may be a serious head injury. When the operator connected him to the nearest Emergency Ward he was told it would be up to two hours before an ambulance could reach them because there were many bad accidents all over the city. Every ambulance was out at the moment.

The look on Jason's face told Stella they had a serious problem, even before he said it would be up to two hours or more before an ambulance could reach them.

"We've got to get to emergency sooner than that. I'm going to get my car, and will take him ourselves. There's no other way. Get your coat on, and bring something we can put over Charles in the backseat of my car."

Jason rushed back across the yard, bolted through his front door, and told Emma what was going on in two sentences. He grabbed his car keys off the desk, and ran out opening the garage with his remote. He carefully drove his car into Charles's driveway, stoping opposite the front door. Stella was still standing at the door. Jason jumped out, and opened the back door of his car. He went past Stella, grabbed Charles under the armpits, and dragged him to the open rear door of his car. He was able to get most of Charles's upper body into the rear seat, then rushed around, opened the door on the other side, reached in, and pulled him all the way onto the seat. Stella laid a blanket over Charles.

It was five miles to the nearest Emergency Ward, and the driving was very slow. When they pulled up to Emergency twenty five minutes later it was still snowing hard. Jason and Stella rushed inside, and got two men to come out with a gurney and wheel Charles inside.

An hour passed before a doctor was free to come check on Charles. "How long has he been unconscious," Dr. Frank asked as he moved to the gurney.

"It's probably been at least two hours," Jason said. "Two hours to two and a half hours."

"That's pretty long, and from the size of this bump on his head, I suspect we have a serious concussion here."

Over the next hour, Dr. Frank and two nurses examined all of Charles's vital signs. He did not stir as they worked on him. Dr. Frank looked seriously concerned. "We are going to need an MRI scan of his wound, and his brain. The bruise on his head is still swelling, I think we have to open that up to avoid undue pressure on his brain. I'm moving him to intensive care. Are you his wife?"

"Yes, I'm his wife Stella. And this is our friend Jason, our neighbor who rescued him when he fell on our driveway getting out of his car. Will he recover Doctor?"

"I think so. His vital signs are okay. You may have saved his life, because if he had staid there in the cold for a few hours he probably would not have survived. Now let me have him moved right away to intensive care. Once he is in intensive care, the two of you will be able to be with him in his room. I'll see you up there shortly. A nurse will be able to tell you the room number."

As the doctor walked away, Stella began to cry. Jason put an arm around her and said, "it will be all right I think, these kinds of injuries can take time to heal, but they almost always do, and leave no lasting damage." They watched as Charles was wheeled into the hallway and onto an elevator. They sat quietly in some nearby chairs, Stella still weeping, Jason with a hand on one of her shoulders. Forty minutes later a nurse came and said, "Charles is in room 308, and you can go there now.'

When they entered that room Stella shrieked when she saw the large bandage on the back left side of Charles's head. Dr. Frank was there, and explained that they had drained the wound, and had it thickly bandaged so there could be additional drainage.

At two in the morning, Stella persuaded Jason to go home. At ten the next morning she called Jason's house.

"Emma, this is Stella, I'm still at the hospital, and Charles is beginning to wake up. He's still very groggy, and has trouble speaking, but Dr. Frank says he will be fine. I imagine Jason has gone to work."

"Yes he has, but I'll call him to tell him the good news. When he left for work he said he will wait until there's some news about Charles before he calls the Mansour bank to tell Bertha, and the others, what has happened to Charles."

"Thank you Emma, Jason really did rescue Charles from death."

The Restaurant Affair in 2010 brought to the Ward a real-life experience with ethnic, religious, economic, and racial hostility.

They learned how to overcome these sources of difficulties so widespread in modern America.

It was a typical quiet, early morning in 2010, on South Street when Akbar looked across the street though the front door of his Monsour Cuisine, an Iraqi restaurant next to the Syrian restaurant. Just then a large Van pulled into the ample parking area beside the large empty building. That building had once been a large dry goods store, but it had been empty, and not well maintained, for at least ten years.

Akbar watched intently when five people exited the Van, which he could now see had "Lake Union Commercial Real Estate" brightly displayed on the side of a front door. Two of the people, a man and a woman, carried notebooks and proceeded to one of the three doors on the front of the building. The woman reached in her purse and took out a key. With some difficulty she got the key to unlock the door so she could push it inward. The five of them stood there talking for at least ten minutes before entering. During that time Akbar cold see the other three people were, as he thought, foreigners—two Asians and one Hispanic. "This may not be a good sign," he says to himself as he walks back to summon his wife to come see what is happening. They stand watching the five people through several front windows in that large, empty store. They could see those people moving around in there inspecting its large space.

"Those people with the notebooks must be the real estate agents, and the foreigners the ones who want to buy, or rent, the place. I don't like this," he says to his wife. In fact, he was very angry, as other store owners on South Street would soon be. They immediately thought of it as an invasion by aliens!

"Don't jump to conclusions, until we meet the people, if indeed they will be opening a store there," his wife Alaha says as the five people come out of the store. "Wait a minute, I think I met all three of those foreign people at the Fourteenth Ward gathering by the Lake last week, and they were great to talk to. Fascinating people, with interesting backgrounds," she says with enthusiasm that really irritates Akbar.

She had met the three people at that community gathering because they all lived in the same block on Crimson Street in the Ward. She said: "I learned they planned to explore establishing a joint Chinese, Japanese and Hispanic restaurant in the Ward. The Chinese woman is Susan Lan Huang. The Japanese guy is Jonathan Shunji Hiroki, and the Hispanic woman is Ana Maria Corvesa. They discovered that by pooling their savings of many years they could afford to buy that large store, and create a restaurant with all three cuisines. They all had prior experience working in restaurants as cooks and waiters, and will name the place "Delights From Three Continents."

Akbar saw the sign go up on the new restaurant the next day. Over the next two days he went to meet with all the owners of the mid-Eastern restaurants and shops on his side of the street. They all agreed to file a complaint with the City, but it was quickly rejected. They laid plans for a lawsuit, but all the lawyers they talked to said any such suit would cost a lot and fail, because the new restaurant was just an exercise of free enterprise under the law—something most leaders in the Ward would welcome.

Hearing about the filed complaint and possible lawsuit, Ana, Susan, and Jonathan went to Akbar to talk about their plans, and why it would increase appeal to more customers for all the restaurants and shops on the street. They pointed to the fact that the Fourteenth Ward was ethnically and racially diverse. Akbar admitted they were correct. He even had several latinos and African Americans on his staff. Ana,

Susan and Jonathan went to talk with the other restaurant and shop owners, and one by one they agreed it was all right.

As the first year passed shop owners on the street increasingly joined together for lunches and dinners. They observed that people from much wider in the Ward as well as numerous customers from many parts of the city, and suburbs, came frequently. Increasingly, Emma and Jason with Barton, and Charles and Stella, came for suppers and lunches in one or another of the Mansour restaurants. Soon more residents of the Ward joined them on a regular basis.

A few long-time restaurant and shop owners were still hoping the new restaurant would fail. It did not, and in fact it was an instant success that improved business for all the restaurants, and shops. The most striking change in the customer clientele was the attracting of many Japanese, Latino and Chinese, as well as Afro-Americans, to all the restaurants and shops—actually not surprising since this diversity had become obvious in the Ward over the last ten years.

And then 2012 came, and the Fight to Save the Fourteenth Ward Schools—Potentially a politically conservative tragedy in the making.

In Barton's third year on Primrose Street, the schools trouble suddenly erupted. Early one morning Barton opened the local paper. Across the top it said in large letters: "IT IS TiME TO REORGANIZE OUR 14th WARD SCHOOLS." As he read the column he was shocked that the city's School Board wanted to eliminate the Fourteenth Ward schools, and share their marvelous success, students, and teachers with all the other schools in the City. The Board declared; "Next year the Fourteenth Ward schools will be closed. A bussing system will relocate all students to other schools throughout the City. All Fourteenth Ward teachers and administrators at every level will be reassigned to other schools throughout the City. We will have a fully integrated system enjoying all the past successes of the Fourteenth Ward schools." Barton had paid little attention to the school board election three years earlier, though he was aware that a conservative majority had been elected.

Barton called Sung, who was now a close friend. "What is this all about?"

"It's a disaster, Barton. Instead of doing the hard work to raise the standards in many of the other schools they are trying to get it on the cheap, and at the expense of many lives in the Fourteenth ward. Most of our kids walk to school. Now they'll be bussed all over, separated from friends. They are trying to ram this through before next year's school board election, because they are afraid the majority on the board might change then."

"Well, I know several of the best lawyers in the Ward," Barton said. "We can halt this crazy action with a lawsuit ASAP!"

"I think that will be the only way, Barton. And another bad thing about this is what it might do to interactions among students and parents in the other schools. One of my colleagues who lives across town said some of his neighbors who saw the paper are already saying things like; 'We don't want all those foreign kids shoved into our schools'."

"Oh Sung. That's disgusting and frightening."

"Yes, and so at odds with what we have in the Ward's schools. Here there is not just tolerance, but celebration of all our diverse racial, ethnic, and cultural backgrounds. I'm convinced it is a source of curiosity that creates excitement and understanding—driving the majority of our elementary and high school students to excel. Not to mention the richness it gives to the lives of our teachers, to all of us.

As it happened, the next weekend was the time of the annual "Fourteenth Ward Lakeside Community Gathering." Hundreds of residents and friends would come for food, games, speeches, used book sales, music, arts and crafts, and more. Barton had his own plan. He knew two of the lawyers in the Ward would be there, and intended to enlist them in the fight to keep their schools. In less than an hour he drew them aside, and in twenty minutes they had a plan to seek an immediate injunction against the School Board's plan. Barton said he would pay all of it, but the two lawyers said it would be a three-way split on the costs, and their own work would be pro bono.

Three months later the School Board, faced with major legal expenses fighting the injunction, and probable loss in court in the end, backed off its plan completely. And new people, including Emma, and others like minded, ran for election and changed the right-wing political composition of the Board.

First attacks by bombers and gunmen came to the Ward in 2014, and after.

In 2014 it was no great surprise when a man and a woman from other parts of the City attacked the Ward. One man bombed the entrance to the high school, and a woman exploded a device on the street in the Monsour district. In those instances no one died except the assailant.

But these armed attacks were enough. The Community Association devised a plan by which certified residents with concealed guns would attend all of the Ward's public gatherings. Eventually, almost a hundred such citizens were enrolled after extensive reviews. Published reports about these measures had the effect of reducing such attacks to only a few over coming years.

One time when this security measure paid off was at the large annual Community Gathering by the Lake in 2018. A man originally from Tennessee ran in with a large automatic rifle yelling; "the end to all you liberal faggots and homos."

As he started to lower his gun toward the crowd two people, Gordon and Maria, pulled out their guns and fired. The man was hit in his right shoulder and left knee, and as he fell backwards his gun fired a couple of automatic shots into the air. As he hit the ground another man, Peter, yanked his rifle away. The police and an ambulance took him away to the hospital in about twenty minutes, during which time the crowd was almost silent with shock. In later discussions that day, and afterward, it was clear that we needed such local protection along with much better gun control nationally.

In 2020 a man who tried to shoot people in the Ward's only movie theater was stopped when two attendants in the lobby there pulled their guns and killed him before he could enter the theater auditorium with an automatic rifle.

Lorita, Looking Ahead, Causes and Effects.

I, Lorita, had long imagined I would eventually write again about the past, present and future of the Fourteenth Ward. On January 1, 2021 I sat down at my computer and began. As a month went by I was surprised how easily the thoughts, memories, and words came. How rapidly the Ward's past sagas, and all the recent issues, and meanings, unfolded.

I'm looking back on my more than forty years living in the Ward, and I want to summarize some major parts of the Ward's recent past. More important, though, is to think about what we face right now, and what will happen in the coming years. Is there hope? Will our special accomplishments and joys continue? The current state of the World and our Country that surrounds us continues to pose serious, and often surprising, even sometimes frightening, challenges.

The development of the Ward from beginning until now has been a river of struggles. But many of the struggles came and went, and at every shifting stage there was progress. Our community became increasingly organized, and to a large extent self-supporting, while at the same time providing multitudes of friendship, sharing, and support for each of us. Great moments came when we defeated attempts by many realtors to control the racial and ethnic diversity of the Ward, and when that wonderful diversity led to our outstanding schools. Schools so outstanding that they gained national recognition, so much so that the School Board once decided to spread our teachers and students all over the Like Union schools, by extensive and complex reassignment and bussing. The Board even debated whether to close our schools completely in that process. We won that hard fought battle, and many others. Some of our greatest moments came at various community meetings, and especially at the annual Ward's celebrations by the Lake. Yes, it has been a river of struggles, but also a river of triumphs, joys, and hopes.

There were many sad moments when some of our people died here in the Ward, and worse when too many younger men and women died in the Afghan War, two different Iraq wars, and earlier in the Vietnam War. Yesterday at a special gathering in the High School Library, Ahmed Lemoont gave this previously arranged talk about the Ward's recent events, and his hopes for our future, as follows:

"All the trials and tribulations we have faced and overcome over many decades have prepared us for great trials coming.

The two ISIS suicide bombings last year by Muslim jihadists from other parts of the City provide one indication of what we face. They decided to attack the Ward, rather than their own places in the City, because they hate things we stand for. Much earlier the bomber at the High School posted a sign just before he ran up killing only himself, and damaging the school's entrance. His sign simply said: 'kill all the blacks, latinos, chinese, muslims, and japs.' The woman who blew herself up in the middle of the street in the Monsour area the same year left something similar in her note. She didn't kill anyone other than herself, but six people walking in front of the shops were injured, and scared people from the shops nevertheless rushed out to help each of them.

"As all of you know there was some criticism in the papers, on radio, and TV of the Ward's large accommodation of migrants: many young children, some parents, and mothers fleeing countries more recently from the Middle East, Africa, and quite a few other places. All of us rejoice over the Ward's receiving, and caring for, these desperate immigrants, and the happiness and diversity it has brought to them, and our neighborhoods, schools, and community. To be blunt, some people in the City hate us for it, though that is not universal by any means. The Ward's Child Care Organization received small monetary contributions from people all over the City. And I heard that as a result of the Ward's project some new organizations started to help more of these refugees in their own neighborhoods in the City. And you recall also how the Ward led the move toward calm reason during the Ebola panic by seeing that the Ward's hospital really prepared for, and did help, a small, but significant number of infected immigrants, returning doctors, and nurses.

"Now, I leave it to all of you, to lead us through a brighter future in the face of all the new wars, warming climate. domestic violence, too many guns, never ending poverty, economic disparity, and the political turmoil in our country, now five years since the end of the fine Obama Presidency. And, I know our people in the Ward will lead us on, just as wonderfully as in the past. Thank you."

In the midst of wild applause, I heard Akbar, standing in the front row, shouting; "right on Ahmed." Akbar's own pilgrimage from his narrow ethnic conceptions based on his loyalty to Monsour Muslim ideals, to his ever broadening ideals about the whole Ward Community, have been amazing to me. He reflects the many eclectic views that have arisen in the lives of so many of us, as the Ward became our model for a greater humanity.

I watched as some people gathered around Ahmed thanking him, while others gathered in smaller groups talking excitedly with each other. No one seemed eager to leave, and I thought again: This is who we have been, and who we still are— an indestructible community of friendships, cooperation, sharing, with an enduring and amazing sense of belonging.

Let us hope the future will not be different, here, and across the world eventually, Or, is this just my wishful thinking. The many awful ideas promulgated in the buildup to our 2016 presidential election: patrolling Muslim neighborhoods, isolating Mexico completely, fostering ever more guns, lobbying against control of continuing climate change, and much more. And now similarly all that has followed for the coming election this year certainly diminish such hopes for America. And all that along with the enduring violence across much of the world does challenge my optimism.

Printed in the United States
By Bookmasters